The Princess and the Potty

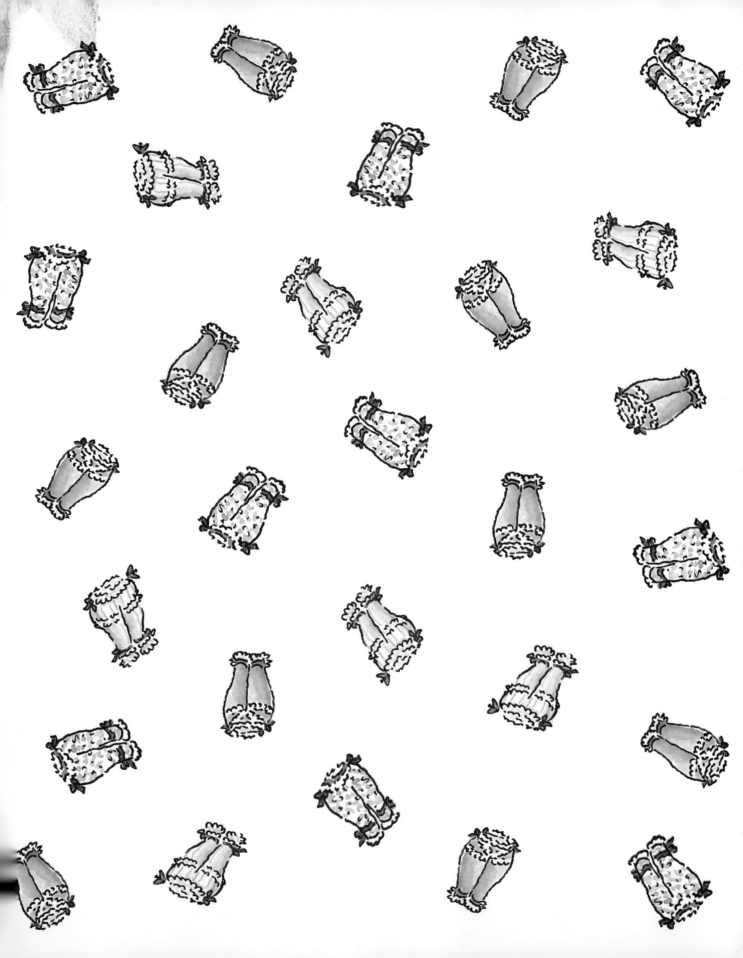

The Princess and the Potty

by Wendy Cheyette Lewison

illustrated by Rick Brown

SCHOLASTIC INC.

New York Toronto London Auckland Sydney
Mexico City New Delhi Hong Kong

Once upon a time there was a princess who wouldn't use her potty.

"This potty doesn't please me,"
said the princess. "Take it away!"

"The potty doesn't please the princess," said
the chambermaid.

"The potty doesn't please the princess," said
the nurserymaid.

So they took away the potty, and the princess
wore her royal diaper instead.

Now the king and queen were not happy
with this. Whoever heard of a princess who
wouldn't use her potty?

What would their neighbors say in the
kingdom next door?

They simply had to find a potty that would please the princess.

So they sent out an urgent request to the finest potty makers in the land.

Soon potties poured into the palace.
First came a pink potty.
"Pink is the princess's favorite color,"
said the potty maker. "A pink potty will
surely please her."

But it didn't.

Then came a purple potty, a yellow potty,

and a polka-dot potty.

One potty maker brought a musical potty.
Another brought a potty that glowed in the dark.

But the princess wasn't interested in any
of these fine potties. She had better things to do.
The king and queen had to try something else.

So they tried singing to the princess and
reading to the princess.

They sent in the princess's royal teddy bear
to keep her company.

They sent in the whole court to keep her company.

Finally, they sat on potties themselves just to show the princess how much fun it was.

The princess laughed and laughed, but she wouldn't use the potty.

Not knowing what else to do, the king and queen sent for the royal wise man to get his advice.

"If you ask me," said the royal wise man, "the princess will use the potty when it pleases her to use the potty."

"And when will that be?" asked the king and queen.

But that was a question that even the royal wise man could not answer.

So they waited and waited for a time to come when it would please the princess to use the potty.

Now one day the princess was watching the queen
get dressed for a grand ball. As the queen bent down
to pull up her royal stockings, the princess noticed
the beautiful pantalettes she had on.

"Those pantalettes please me," said the princess.

The very next day the queen took the princess shopping. They picked out the prettiest pair of pantalettes in the land—pantalettes fit for a princess!

The princess wore them all the way home
to the palace.

She wore them all the way through playtime.

She wore them all the way through her snack of milk and cookies.

Suddenly, the princess could not sit still. She sat this way and she sat that way. She crossed her legs. She got down on her knees.

"She needs her royal diaper!" cried the king to the chambermaid.

"She needs her royal diaper!" cried the queen to the nurserymaid.

But the princess did not want her royal diaper. She would have had to take off her pretty new pantalettes to put it on. And that she did not want to do.

"I NEED MY POTTY!" cried the princess.

The royal servants ran to get every potty
in the palace.

But the princess chose the plain one
because it was the nearest.
"This potty pleases me," said the princess.

And so it did.

For my daughter, Elizabeth Anne Lewison—WCL
For Lauren—RB

ISBN 0-439-10669-9

Text copyright © 1994 by Wendy Cheyette Lewison.
Illustrations copyright © 1994 by Rick Brown. All rights reserved.
Published by Scholastic Inc., 555 Broadway, New York, NY 10012,
by arrangement with Aladdin Paperbacks, an imprint of
Simon & Schuster Children's Publishing Division. SCHOLASTIC and
associated logos are trademarks and/or registered trademarks of Scholastic Inc.

12 11 10 9 8 7 6 5 4 3 2 1   9/9 0 1 2 3 4/0

Printed in the U.S.A.   24

First Scholastic printing, September 1999

The text for this book was set in 20 point Kennerly.

The illustrations were done in ink and watercolor.

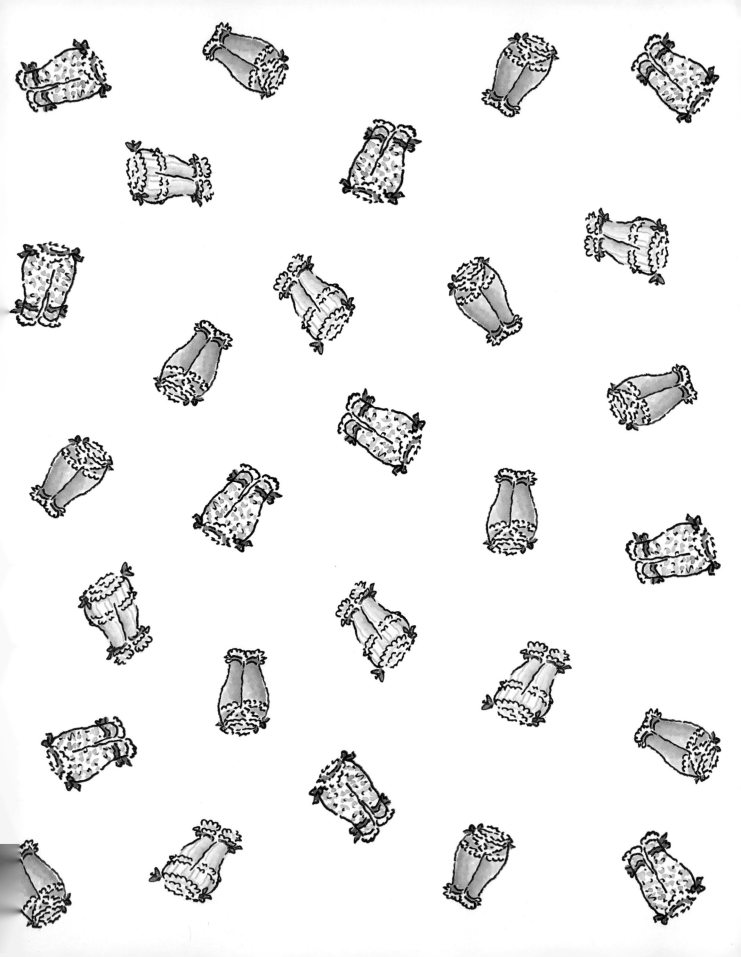

WENDY CHEYETTE LEWISON has written many books for young children, including *Going to Sleep on the Farm*, a Bank Street College "Children's Book of the Year." About *The Princess and the Potty*, she had this to say:

"I dedicated this book to my daughter, Elizabeth, because she knows what she wants and does not want in life. At age three, she did not want to be potty trained. This was a problem for me, because the local nursery school wouldn't accept her in diapers. But a lot *she* cared. To have her out of diapers in time, I had to quickly come up with something that 'Princess Elizabeth' *would* care about. And after reading this book, you all know what that was. . . . "

Ms. Lewison has had a varied career as a teacher, editor, and writer. She and her husband, John, live in Westchester County, New York. Their two children, Elizabeth and David, are grown up now and have potties of their own.

RICK BROWN is the illustrator of more than two dozen books for children. His first book, *Even the Devil Is Afraid of a Shrew*, was chosen as one of the Children's Books of the Year by the American Institute of Graphic Artists. More recently *Rockabye Farm* was chosen as one of the Best Books of 1992 by *Parents* magazine. Other titles include the Porkchop books by Susan Pearson and the Kate travel books by Pat Brisson.

"At first I was reluctant to take on *The Princess and the Potty*. I was not sure I wanted to do a book about that nasty subject. My wife, Lynne, read over the manuscript and with her approval and some gentle coaxing from the editor, I decided to take on the project. I'm pleased with the way everything turned out, so to speak!"